The Hare and the Moon

A calming fable
for anxious children

Written and illustrated by

Sophie Shaw

ISBN: 978-1-0993-2340-9

The Hare and the Moon

For Barney

1.

Once long ago, a hare and a tortoise decided to have a race.
Do you know the story? It goes like this...

Hare was young, enthusiastic and simply bursting with energy. He was a very fast runner, so he was sure that he could easily beat the Tortoise. He was so confident in fact, that he decided to take a short nap during the race.

This was a mistake, for unfortunately he fell fast asleep, and while he slept, the Tortoise plodded slowly past him and across the finish line! All the other animals had gathered to watch the race and they roared with laughter.

Hare was so embarrassed. He felt very foolish. He had been very boastful about his brilliant speed and all his friends teased him.

The snooty Fox looked down his long nose at Hare and said, "That'll teach you to brag, you silly hare".

Wasn't that unkind?

SOPHIE
SHAW

Hare couldn't understand it – he had spent all spring racing his friends across the meadow and he'd beaten every one of them. How could this have happened?

He loped off to his home under the big, broad oak tree. His mother was waiting for him there and at once she saw his sadness and confusion. She made him a special supper of dandelion leaves and parsley, but Hare couldn't eat – not even one bite. Off he went and curled up in his little nest, feeling very sorry for himself.

The sun began to sink low behind the trees, the shadows got longer in the grass and Hare felt more and more downhearted with every passing moment.

He began to worry.

"What does this mean?" he thought to himself. "Am I a terrible runner?"

Running was his favourite thing to do. He loved the feeling of the wind rushing through his fur; his strong back legs driving him powerfully onwards; his soft paws bounding off the warm earth and the wet grass.

Running, running, running – there was nothing like it!

"What will I do if I can't run any more?" he said to himself.

Then Hare thought of his friends and of the nasty Fox - how they had all laughed at him. "They must not like me anymore," he thought in dismay. Would they all be talking about him now and saying mean things? Hare couldn't bear to think of it.

His mind was filled with worries and he began to feel afraid. He looked about him - and all at once he thought he saw faces out in the darkness, unkind and angry.

SOPHIE
SHAW

He felt a dull sickness in his tummy, his fur stood up on end and he began to tremble. His heart drummed speedily, like a tiny hare running hard in his chest. He remembered the haughty Fox and imagined he could hear his cruel laugh.

He buried his face in his paws and cried out in fear. His mother, hearing his cries, sprang to him at once.

"Whatever is the matter?" she asked with great concern.

"There are scary faces out there," he sobbed. "Nobody likes me anymore, and I can't run, and Fox is going to get me, and – and –"

“Shh, shh…” whispered Mother Hare. “The dark plays tricks, there’s no-one there, I promise you.”

Hare wasn’t so sure.

“I know what we should do,” continued Mother Hare. “Let’s go and talk to the Moon.”

Hare looked up at his mother, confused. He sniffed.

“The Moon?” he asked, tears slipping off the ends of his whiskers.

“Oh yes. It’s time for you to learn who we are. Come with me, my love.”

2.

Despite his fear, Hare was intrigued - he had never left the safety of the great oak at night before. He followed his mother as she padded softly out from under the spread of its arms. The darkness lay thickly all around them and Hare nervously hid behind his paws.

Led by his mother's guiding touch, they came to a stop after a few short hops.

"My son, let me tell you a tale," she began.

SOPHIE
SHAW

"It is said that long ago, when the world was new, all the animals and birds roamed the earth without a purpose. The beasts walked the land in all directions, going they knew not where; the birds flew about carelessly, and the oceans were filled with aimless creatures."

"Then, in the night sky, appeared the moon and the north star. In the daylight sky, came the sun, the cloud-mountains and the rainbows. Across the land there grew rivers, waterfalls, mountains and valleys. The world was filled with beauty and wonder, and every creature found something in it to love and to inspire them."

SOPHIE
SHAW

Hare listened, fascinated - yet he kept his eyes still closed behind his paws.

Mother Hare continued:

“The day-birds worshipped the cloud-mountains, for they flew among them. The night-birds loved the stars and they were forever trying to reach them. Otters fell in love with the running rivers, of course – and it is said that the very first hare fell in love with the Moon - and she with him. They made a promise that they would love one other for as long as they lived.”

“Well, the Moon cannot die - so the first Hare loved her until the very end of his time on earth, and then he joined her in the sky to live with her there forever after.

SOPHIE SHAW

She promised him that she would watch over his family, and all their descendants, until the end of time.

“From that day to this, we have been Moon-gazing hares. She watches over us still.”

Mother Hare paused, quietly.

“She is with us tonight. Would you like to meet her?”

Burning with curiosity, Hare peeked out from behind his paws and saw that a gentle silvery light now bathed the leaves and grass all around him. The angry faces had disappeared, and the night meadow was peaceful and quiet.

Hare swallowed hard. He sniffed the air. It smelled sweet, like grass in summer. He smelled the warm bark of the big oak tree nearby and felt its soft, dry leaves on the ground beneath him.

"Look up," said Mother Hare.

Hare slowly raised his head a little. He still felt afraid. He looked up into the wide arms of the great oak, but he saw nothing except leaves and branches.

"Wh-where is she?" he stuttered.

"Look up," whispered Mother Hare once more.

So, Hare summoned all his courage, sat up on his big back legs and looked all the way up into the night sky.

His mouth fell open in astonishment.

To his amazement, he saw a huge, silvery white circle shining up there like a great lamp. It was so beautiful that he couldn't take his eyes off it.

At that moment, he thought he heard a gentle whisper:

"Be still. Have courage. All is well."

He turned to his mother - she had not spoken, but she was smiling. Where had that voice come from?

"I am with you. Be still. Have courage. All is well."

"Who said that?" he asked.

His mother simply turned her face to the night sky and gazed upwards at the Moon, a peaceful expression on her face.

"I am the Moon," said a sweet voice. "I am with you. All is well."

Hare looked up. The silver disc glowed brilliantly, casting its light across the sky.

"What should I do?" he asked.

Mother Hare remained quiet.

"Be still," the Moon seemed to say.

Hare gazed up at the Moon - his body had stopped trembling and he became still. He felt his heartbeat begin to slow and his fur started to settle down at last.

"How long must I be still?" he asked. But the Moon was silent.

Hare's thoughts raced noisily in his mind, but he said nothing. Instead he waited, gazing up into the Moon's beautiful, shining face – and as he waited, something extraordinary began to happen.

SOPHIE
HAW

His thoughts began to quieten and slow down. The more he sat still and looked at the Moon, the calmer he felt. The more he focussed on her simple beauty, the less he thought about his worries. He forgot to feel afraid and instead he felt warm and peaceful. Eventually he felt completely at ease, and ready for sleep.

He turned to his mother, who smiled deeply at him, her whiskers sparkling in the moonlight. They hopped gently back to their nests and within moments, Hare fell into a deep and comfortable sleep.

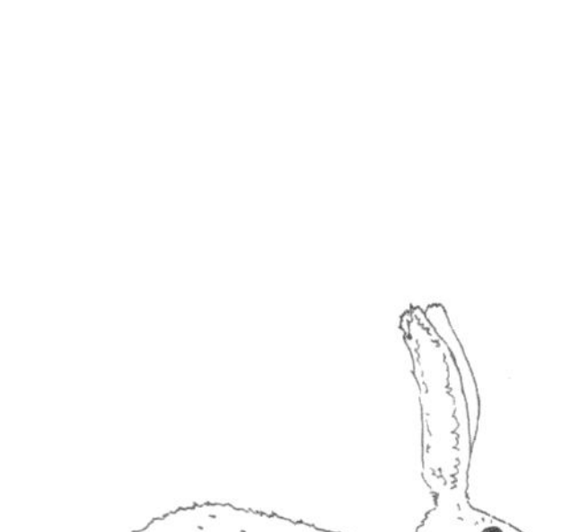

3.

The next morning Hare woke late, yawned and stretched his long legs. His mother had already left the nest and gone for breakfast. It was a beautiful day and the sky was clear, open and blue. He hopped a little way out of his leafy bed and began to nibble on a bright yellow dandelion that bloomed close by. The little petals went up his nose, tickling him and making his nose twitch. He grinned.

Just then he began to remember what had happened the day before – how he had lost the race and been embarrassed in front of everyone. How the other animals had laughed, how Fox had sneered and how alone and afraid he had felt.

He started to feel uneasy again and he worried what the other animals would say when he saw them. Would they be mean to him? He felt his heart begin to beat against his chest and his fur began to prickle. He felt that dull sickness in his tummy once more and stopped eating his dandelion.

SOPHIE SHAW

Across the meadow, he could see a group of his friends chasing each other through the grass, playing happily. He was afraid to face them.

He dropped his head, flattened his ears and took off running in the other direction at full speed. He heard them calling after him:

"Hare! Come and play!"

"Where are you going?"

"Hare, come back!"

But he just kept running as fast as he could.

All morning Hare sped across the meadows, over fields and under hedges - running, running, running until he was exhausted. Finally, he plopped down under a hawthorn bush and caught his breath. He felt utterly miserable. Running was usually his favourite thing, but he couldn't stop thinking about the race and the other animals.

His tummy still ached, and he still felt trembly and worried. He didn't know what he was going to do.

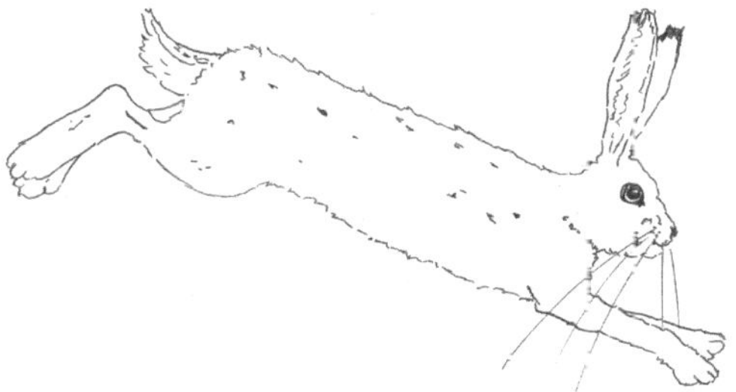

Just then, he remembered the Moon and he looked up into the bright sky to find her. He couldn't see the Moon anywhere, just the Sun shining above him, as usual. It was so dazzling that Hare couldn't look at it. The Moon was nowhere to be seen. She must have gone.

Hare whispered to himself "Oh Moon, where are you?"

"I am with you," came a soft reply.

Surprised, Hare looked up again. There wasn't a single cloud in the sky for the Moon to hide behind - where could she be?

"I can't see you, Moon – are you there?" called Hare.

"Look within. I am with you," she seemed to reply.

"Within?" repeated the Hare, "Within where?" But the Moon was silent.

So Hare began to look for her. He searched everywhere; within bushes, within hedges, even within the burrow of the very grumpy Badger, who shooed him out impatiently. He looked all afternoon but couldn't find her anywhere. Dejected and exhausted, he plodded slowly home.

SOPHIE
SHAW

“Where have you been? I haven’t seen you all day!” his mother said, when she saw him.

“I was looking for the Moon. I – I think she’s gone,” answered Hare, tears stinging his eyes.

Mother Hare tipped her head to one side and looked at her son, thoughtfully.

“Moon will never leave us, my love. Sometimes we have to look within to find her.”

“I did! I looked within everything I could see!” he cried.

Mother Hare tried not to smile. “Oh, my sweet one - you looked hard, didn’t you?” she said, kindly. “Perhaps it’s time for a little rest.”

Tired out, Hare went and sat down under a foxglove and closed his eyes. He thought about the Moon and remembered what she had said:

"Be still. Have courage. I am with you. All is well."

Where was she, then?

He thought about her luminous face and her gentle words. He could see her in his imagination, her glowing roundness and the softness of her voice. He began to remember how he had felt, gazing up at her the night before. He started to feel a little calmer. His thoughts began to quieten and slow down.

All at once he realised where she was - he had found her within his mind.

The more he sat still and thought about the Moon, the calmer he felt. The more he focussed on her simple beauty, the less he thought about his worries. He forgot to feel afraid and instead he felt warm and peaceful.

He thought about his friends. Now that he felt calmer, he realised that they were just having fun with him. They often teased one another when they were playing – there was no need for him to feel afraid. He decided to go and find them.

When he reached the long meadow, Hare found his friends waiting there for him.

"Hare! There you are!" they said happily, "Come and play, before the sun goes!" They had clearly forgotten all about the race. Hare sighed with relief and together they chased each other across the meadow until the shadows grew long and their mothers called them home.

SOPHIE
HAW

4.

Later that evening, Hare stepped into his leafy bed and got himself ready for sleep. He brushed his long ears with his front paws, shook out his fur, curled himself into a little ball and waited for sleep to come. Night bugs hummed, the meadow was peaceful, and Hare grew drowsy.

Just as he was drifting quietly off, Hare suddenly thought of Fox and his harsh words. He pictured Fox's snooty face and the curl of his lip as he sneered down at him. All at once, Hare was wide awake. His heart was racing and even though he was perfectly warm, he began to shiver. His tummy ached again, and his fur prickled and stood on end.

He sat up and stared out into the darkness. Was Fox out there somewhere waiting for him? He could feel the frightened tears building in his eyes. He looked into the shadows, straining his eyes to see what was out there. He tensed his long ears, listening for any sound.

Crickets chirruped. A gentle breeze blew through the meadow grass and lightly stirred the oak leaves overhead. Beyond that, all was still.

At that moment, he heard a familiar whisper in his mind:

"Be still. Have courage. I am with you. All is well."

His heart leapt and he looked straight up into the inky blackness of the sky overhead. There was the Moon, shimmering brightly above him. Hare sighed with relief.

"Moon." he breathed. He became still.

He noticed that the Moon was a little smaller tonight, as if a slice had been taken from her side. Despite this, she beamed down at him, bathing him in the glow of her light. Hare gazed up at her; he couldn't take his eyes off her shining face.

SOPHIE
SHAW

Without the Moon saying another word, his heartbeat began gently to slow down, and his tummy-ache gradually eased. Hare gazed up at the Moon for a long time, saying nothing all the while, and eventually he felt completely peaceful and content.

The night was still and quiet. Hare lay down once more and very soon drifted into a deep and untroubled sleep.

5.

In the morning, Hare woke up full of energy; he stretched out his long legs so far, that he accidentally kicked his mother awake too. She had been fast asleep, so she grumbled at him, playfully cuffed his ears and sent him off to find breakfast.

He hopped out of his nest and into the sunshine of another beautiful day. The grass beneath his paws was a bright emerald green, speckled with dewdrops that shone like diamonds in the early morning light. It smelled rich and sweet and Hare began to nibble hungrily.

He was soon joined by his friends. They chatted eagerly about their plans for the day and began chasing each other across the meadow, pretending to box and bouncing high in the air. They laughed happily as they ran helter-skelter in all directions. Hare felt playful, with a new spring in his step; he joined in eagerly, leaping higher than ever before. He was full of energy once again.

He noticed one of the younger hares wasn't joining in, but instead was sitting to one side, looking nervous. He hopped over to the youngster and asked him what was wrong.

SOPHIE
SHAW

“I don’t really like the running and boxing,” said the little hare, frowning and gnawing on his lip. “I’m afraid I’ll get hurt.”

Hare raised an eyebrow in surprise. So, he wasn’t the only one with worries! An idea came to him and he smiled broadly.

“Let me tell you a story about the Moon…” he began.

***

Later, when he was alone, Hare thought of Fox. His tummy gave an unpleasant leap, but he didn't feel sick. His heart beat a little faster, but the tiny hare in his chest didn't race hard, it merely skipped along. His fur prickled, but it didn't stand on end.

Hare knew what to do. He closed his eyes and he thought of the Moon. At once he saw her lovely face within his imagination. He felt the glow of her light bathing his fur and he felt peace wash over him like warm summer rain.

A thought came to him. Fox was no friend of his, in fact he was well known for being the rudest of creatures - that was just Fox's way. Most of the other animals ignored him when he behaved that way, so why couldn't Hare ignore him too? As soon as he had this thought, he felt even better. And that evening, when he saw Fox at dinner, Hare was even able to smile pleasantly at him. Fox's look of surprise made Hare smile to himself.

That night, he waited for the Moon. When she appeared, shining above him, she looked even smaller than the night before, but still just as beautiful. They gazed at one another wordlessly for a long time until Hare could no longer keep his eyes open and he drifted easily to sleep.

SOPHIE
SHAW

6.

Over the next few nights, the Moon continued to shrink until eventually she was half her size, though she remained as graceful and radiant as ever.

One night, just before bedtime, Hare asked his mother why she grew smaller every night.

"Remember what I told you?" she asked. "Moon will never leave us, my love. She is merely watching over all the hares on the other side of the sky. She will return, you wait and see."

So, Hare waited, patiently. The Moon shrank further and further, until one night she was completely invisible. But just as his mother had promised, she returned the very next evening, and began to grow again.

Every night, he would be lulled to sleep by her gentle light – and every day, when she could no longer be seen, Hare would spend a little time alone to be still and quietly gaze at the Moon within his mind.

***

One sunny morning, Hare awoke and looked up into the bright, cloudless sky. To his astonishment he saw the Moon there, pale and shining gently.

"I am with you," she said.

Hare was thrilled to see the Moon in the vivid blue of the daytime sky. He was busy all morning, but from time to time he would look up to check she was still there, watching over him. By the afternoon she had disappeared once more, but by now Hare knew where to find her – he looked within.

SOPHIE SHAW

Sometimes Hare saw the Moon during the day and sometimes only at night. Sometimes she shrank away and disappeared completely from the sky, but it was only ever for a short while, and then she grew into a great, glowing circle once more.

Hare knew she would always come back. He knew that she was always there, even if he couldn't see her. He knew that she was always with him. He remembered her words:

"I am with you. Be still. Have courage. All is well."

7.

One late autumn day many years later, when he had grown old and wise, and the leaves of his great oak were turning red and gold, Hare lay down in his soft, dry nest. He had lived a happy and contented life and now he was tired. He thought of his old friend the Moon and smiled quietly to himself.

It was time.

SOPHIE
SHAW

Hare closed his eyes and drifted gently off into a deep and peaceful sleep from which he never awoke. He had gone to be with the Moon at last.

And to this day, if you look up into the night sky, you might see him there, running, running, running with his friend, the beautiful, shining Moon.

Can you see him?

THE END

Do you remember what Mother Hare said? The Moon is always with us, even if we can't see it. Sometimes the Moon looks full and round; sometimes it's just a crescent, and sometimes it disappears completely – but it always comes back again. It's called waxing (getting bigger) and waning (getting smaller).

This cycle is known as the Phases of the Moon – and it looks like this:

Perhaps you'd like to learn how to calm yourself down too?

Here are some questions to help you - write or draw your answers in the spaces below.

Who are your favourite people? Why?

What are your top three favourite toys or belongings? What do you love about them?

Where are you the happiest? What places help you to feel calm and comforted? At home? In school? At the beach?

What's the best advice you've ever been given?

What does it feel like when you are worried or anxious?

When you're worried or anxious, what happens in your body? Does your heart race? Do you tense your muscles? What else?

What things usually make you feel anxious?

When you're feeling anxious, how would you like to feel instead? What would that feel like?

What do you like to do to relax?

Can you picture your favourite place in your imagination? Fill it with beautiful, bright colours and happy sounds, so it really comes to life in your mind.

How do you feel when you are thinking about your favourite place?

What happens in your body?

How long can you hold that picture in your mind?

Can you imagine it for a full minute?

Even longer?

Calming Activities

By now, you're beginning to see that it's just the pictures we make in our minds that make us feel either good or bad, aren't you?

Try the following activities to change the pictures in your mind to ones that feel good!

Your Favourite Place

This takes a little practice – you can do it!

1. Try sitting somewhere comfortably, closing your eyes and imagining your lovely, comforting place.

2. See yourself in that place, happy and smiling – maybe you're even laughing?

3. What favourite clothes are you wearing?

4. Make all the colours bright and vivid in your imagination.

5. Make all the sounds clear.

6. What sort of things can you see? What can you hear? What can you feel?

7. Notice how you feel as you explore the scene in your mind. Notice yourself feeling calmer.

8. Practise imagining for a little longer each time. Start with 15 seconds, then the next time try 30 seconds, then 45 seconds and so on.

Breathe Easy

Have you noticed that when you're very worried or anxious you might forget how to breathe normally? Try this to get your breathing under control.

1. Imagine a big, beautiful balloon at your lips, ready to be blown up – what colour is it?

2. Imagine that you are blowing all your worries into that balloon to inflate it.

3. Use long, slow breaths to blow up your balloon – really fill it up.

4. This balloon can get as BIG as you need it to, so keep blowing until you've emptied all your worries into it and your breathing is nice and calm again.

5. Now let it go, and watch it float off up into the sky.

6. Imagine it floating higher and higher, further and further away, until it becomes a speck in the distance – and then disappears completely.

Going to the Movies

Do you have something that you're particularly afraid of or worried about?

Try this activity to change the pictures in your mind – you can do this for yourself, or you can get someone to talk you through the steps if you like.

1. Imagine sitting in front of a big cinema screen in the comfiest seat ever.

2. The lights dim, and the movie starts. It's a movie about the thing you're feeling most worried about.

3. Maybe you start to feel worried or anxious – BUT – you have the remote control!

4. Pause the movie. All the sound stops, and the picture is frozen.

5. Fast-forward the movie all the way to end – watch everything in your movie crazily rushing around. Now rewind it all the way to the beginning and see everyone ridiculously dashing about backwards. Don't they look silly?

6. Pause it again. What can you see on the screen? Is the picture in colour? Let all the colour drain out of it until it's completely black and white. Now let the picture fade completely – make it grow paler and paler until it fades out completely.

7. Now find the 'shrink' button on your remote control and shrink the screen – make it smaller and smaller until it's tiny enough to hold in your hand.

8. Finally, throw it away! Throw it with all your strength so that it completely disappears off into the distance and you can't see it anymore.

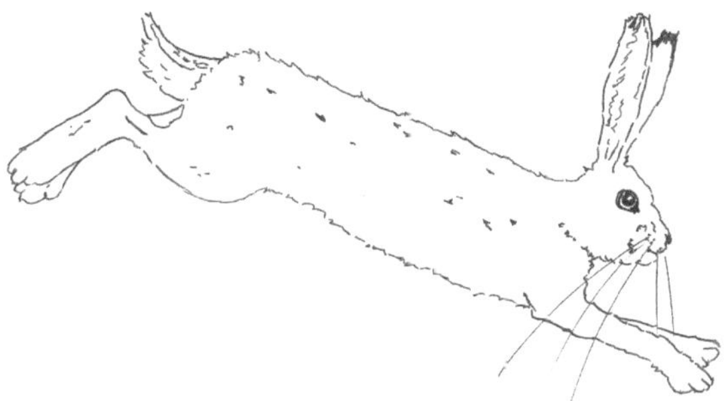

Drawing and colouring can be very relaxing

Try colouring in the pictures on the following pages. Or perhaps you might like to draw your own pictures? What animals do you like? Or maybe you could you draw your comforting person, place or thing?

Colour in scared Hare. How does he feel?

Draw your own picture of feeling scared or worried – what does that look like?

Colour in wise old Hare. What has he learned?

Draw your own picture of someone wise – maybe you when you're older?

What advice would you give to someone with worries?

Colour in happy Hare – what is he thinking about?

How does he feel?

Draw yourself in your own happy place. Use your favourite colours. How does that feel?

Colour in sleeping Hare –
I wonder what he's dreaming about?

Draw your own happy dream –
imagine there are no limits!

About the Author

Sophie Shaw is a hypnotherapist, artist, and Reiki Master Teacher. For over ten years she has been helping her clients to manage their anxiety, stress and difficult emotions, so that they can lead happier lives.

Sophie lives in the wild green of the beautiful Norfolk countryside with her brilliant son, naughty dog and over-confident cat.

Inspired by the healing power of the natural world, The Hare and the Moon is a magical fable about using mindfulness techniques and simple imagination to overcome your fears. It is the first in the Tales of Wonder and Wellbeing series.

The tales are intended to help children feel more confident and to give them comfort and reassurance, as well as giving them tools and techniques that help them manage their difficult emotions.

To be notified when each book is released, please visit **www.sophieshaw.co.uk.** You can also find me on Facebook at **www.facebook.com/sophieshawheals** - or just search for **Sophie Shaw – Hypnotherapy & Wellbeing.**

★★★★★

If you enjoyed this book, can I ask a favour? Would you be kind enough to leave me a review on Amazon? Hare says thank you very much – and so do I!"

Lightning Source UK Ltd.
Milton Keynes UK
UKHW051022080222
398346UK00006B/203